Mary Plain goes to America

*Mary Plain's family are real bears, the
bears that can be seen in zoos.
Mary Plain herself is rather extraordinary
and unusual, even for a bear! Her
adventures have never before appeared in
paperback form, though she has been
a top favourite with children and their
parents for over forty years. The new
illustrations have been specially drawn
by Janina Ede.*

*Other stories about Mary Plain
available in Knight Books are*
MOSTLY MARY
ALL MARY
MARY PLAIN ON HOLIDAY
MARY PLAIN AND THE TWINS
MARY PLAIN'S BIG ADVENTURE
MARY PLAIN V.I.P.

D1421850

Gwynedd Rae

Mary Plain
goes to America

Illustrated by JANINA EDE

KNIGHT BOOKS
the paperback division of Brockhampton Press

ISBN 0 340 14906 X

This edition first published 1971 by Knight Books,
the paperback division of Brockhampton Press Ltd, Leicester

First published 1957 by Routledge & Kegan Paul Ltd
Second impression 1964
© by Routledge & Kegan Paul Ltd
Illustrations copyright © 1971 by Brockhampton Press Ltd

Printed and bound in Great Britain by
Cox & Wyman Ltd, London, Reading and Fakenham

Contents

Introduction.

THIS book is once more about Mary Plain, the real
live bear who came from the bear-pits at Berne. This
latest book tells all about her short visit to America. As
one of her young friends out there said, 'Mary is a
smart guy' and she certainly seems to have packed a
lot of her unusual adventures into her time. Her
friends will agree with me that it is as well for Mary's
character that she had no idea that her visit to Hollywood turned her into its latest star.

GWYNEDD RAE

One · Which begins with a fire and ends with an invitation

'TINGALING! Tingaling!'

Mary sat up in bed, yawned widely and rubbed her eyes.

'Tingaling! Tingaling!'

Mary's ears pricked. That was the telephone, of course. She switched on the light and trotted out into the hall. The telephone sounded in an awful hurry but not nearly as much as the voice that shrilled at her from the other end.

'Is that the Fire Station?' it said. 'Quick! Help! Fire!'

The voice said something that sounded like 'Two-abercorncrescent and better comeatoncelikelightning-or –'

'Pardon?' interrupted Mary.

'Bottom flat – hurry!' shrieked the voice and rang off.

Mary scratched her head. Then she went into the sitting-room and, pushing up the window, leaned out, but she could see no sign of flames.

'Any fire down there?' she called.

'Here!' cried Briar, the porter's cat, mistaking 'Fire' for his own name. He hated being shut out at night and was longing to get in for his early morning saucer of milk, so he, too, shouted, 'Hurry!'

Well, thought Mary, they both said hurry. I'd better tell the Owl Man, and she went off to his room.

But all she could see was a big hump of blanket.

'Fire!' said Mary, looking hopefully at the hump, but nothing happened. That was no good, so she decided to go down and see for herself.

She let herself out of the front door and there, facing her, were two buckets, one of water and one of sand with 'FIRE' printed on them in big black letters. But they were far too heavy for her to carry down all those stairs. Suddenly Mary had a brain-wave and began dragging the sand bucket towards the open door of the flat. Quite a bit of sand went overboard but at last she got it to the sitting-room window and, with a terrific heave, up on to the sill. She could still hear Briar mewing, so she leaned out and called 'Here it comes – look out!'

Unfortunately, Briar, thinking it was his milk, looked up just as the sand fell.

His mews stopped at once.

Probably that meant the fire was out, thought

Mary, but to be on the safe side, she dragged the water bucket, slop, slop across the hall and sent it over the same way. She listened with her head on one side. No more mews from Briar, no more tingalinging from the telephone, so the fire must be out. Mary went back to bed and to sleep.

She was awakened again by a bell, but this time it was the front door and someone was keeping their finger on the push button.

'Another fire!' decided Mary and, rushing out, she nearly collided with the Owl Man, who was hurrying to the door, too. When she saw this, Mary stopped rushing and went and stood behind him.

The Owl Man opened the front door and there stood the hall porter with his arms full of something brown and dripping. Mary took one peep and tucked herself closer in behind the Owl Man.

'Do you know anything about this?' he inquired in an angry voice, holding it out.

'I most certainly do not,' said the Owl Man, stepping back and nearly treading on Mary's paws. 'What is it?'

'Briar,' said the porter.

'Mew!' said Briar, to confirm this.

'Knocked out he was,' continued the porter, 'flat out!'

'Mew!' echoed Briar.

'But, my dear good man,' said the Owl Man, 'I'm

sure I'm sorry if your cat's been half buried' (which was a lie, for Briar was an unlovable animal, and he would have much rather he had been completely buried), 'but why come to me?'

'Because,' said the porter, 'the water and sand came from this floor. See?'

The Owl Man laughed an unamused laugh. 'There are four flats on this floor,' he said. 'Why should you imagine that –' but here he broke off, for the porter had moved aside and was pointing to a trail of sand and water which led from the top of the stairs to his front door. Looking down, the Owl Man saw it continued across his own hall.

'Oh!' said the Owl Man.

'See?' said the porter.

'Miaow!' wailed Briar.

'It was me!' said Mary, who knew when the game was up, and she stepped out from behind the Owl Man. 'The telephone rang and rang. And someone said Fire! Hurry! Bottom flat! and you were asleep and I thought the water would get there quicker if I put it through the window. I'm sorry I spilt it on Briar.'

'Miaow!' said Briar, sourly.

It took a few shillings to calm the porter and three saucers of milk to calm Briar and after that the Owl Man had a bath and a shave while Mary tried her best to clear up the mess. The Owl Man did not scold

Mary because he knew that, once again, she had done her rather upsetting best.

The telephone rang again during breakfast and the Owl Man went off to answer it.

Meanwhile, Mary got on with her porridge. Privately, she was feeling rather bubbly inside. After all, it was not every cub who could put out a fire that wasn't there and knock out a mewing cat from a top-floor window.

'Was it a fire again?' she inquired when the Owl Man returned.

'Not this time,' he answered. 'We've had enough fires for one day. No, I've got to go to the United States next week,' and he sighed a big sigh.

'What are they?' asked Mary.

'The United States of America, to give them their full name.'

'Spell them, please,' said Mary, who had moved up one place in her spelling class at school and was very anxious to reach the top. Mary liked tops best. She went and stood by the Owl Man's knee and watched him write USA on the back of an envelope.

'Why, it's quite a little name!' said Mary, surprised.

'A little name for a big country,' smiled the Owl Man.

'What day do we go?' asked Mary, going back to her seat.

'I don't remember saying anything about your going, Mary.'

'But –' said Mary.

The Owl Man shook his head and Mary pushed her plate away and her ears drooped dismally.

'Why?' she asked.

'Because, you see,' said the Owl Man, gently, because of the ears, 'you have to have an invitation to go to the States and you haven't been invited.'

Mary's head went down, too. 'Do you think the twins are happy without me?' she said, in her smallest voice of all.

This was a question that Mary only asked when she was unhappy and remembered her twin cousins in the bear-pits at Berne.

'That's an idea!' exclaimed the Owl Man. 'How would you like to pay them a visit while I'm away?'

Mary shook her head. 'I like it with you best.'

The Owl Man looked at his watch. He hated leaving Mary all of a droop, but he just had to get to his office. 'I must fly,' he said. 'We'll go for a run in the park when I get back and I shan't be late. Cheer up, old girl!'

But the old girl just couldn't. As the front door closed behind him she sat down on a little stool in the hall with her head between her paws. All the bubbly feeling had gone. Her ears drooped, so did her head

and her heart felt as if it were down in her paws. But after just two minutes, everything suddenly went up again and Mary clapped her paws.

She ran to the sitting-room desk and scrambled up into the Owl Man's revolving chair. This chair always fascinated Mary, so she had a few spins in it as a beginning; then she pulled out a sheet of stamped paper and, breathing heavily, with her tongue following the course of the pen, she wrote a letter. Then she addressed an envelope, stamped it, had a few more spins to end up with and going out of the front door, posted it through their own letter-box.

That done, she went back to the stool and stared fixedly at the front door, hardly moving till she heard the Owl Man's key in the lock.

Mary's heart went pit-a-pat as he came in.

'Good!' he said, thankful to see Mary's ears were in the right position again. 'Hallo! Here's a letter,' and he stooped and picked it up. When he saw the writing he looked at Mary over the top of his spectacles, but she had her back turned and, with two paws clasped behind her back, was kicking the mat with another.

'Let's go and see what it says, shall we?' suggested the Owl Man and went and sat on the sitting-room sofa. Mary stood very close to him while he opened it. It was written in Mary writing.

Mary laid her tightly clasped paws on the Owl Man's knees. 'I've got one now, haven't I?' she asked.

The Owl Man took a deep breath and then smiled his nicest smile.

'All right, Mary. You win!'

Two · Mary prepares for a flying visit to America

MARY sighed loudly. It was not her fault that her inky paw made too big a splotch on the visa paper. She and the Owl Man were at the American Embassy getting their passport visas for the United States and they could not get the visas without the finger-prints. It was a hot August day – the last kind of day you would choose for such a business. The Owl Man felt very sorry for Mary but not nearly as sorry as Mary felt for herself as she stood on an immense sheet of blotting-paper.

'The left hind paw again, please, Miss Plain,' said the young American finger-printer and his smile was a good deal less kind than it had been twenty minutes ago.

Now, a hind paw is awkward to reach and Mary had suggested standing on her head so that he could get at it better, but the man insisted on kneeling on the floor and steadying the bowl of ink at arm's length.

'Hustle!' he said briefly.

So, for the third time and with a slight shudder, Mary dipped her paw into the ink and plopped it on to the paper.

The young man picked up the paper and sighed. It looked exactly as if someone had upset a bottle of ink and then sat down in it by mistake. 'It will have to do,' he said gloomily.

'I hope so,' said the Owl Man, 'because if we're here much longer I should think there's every danger of the ship sailing without us.' He was getting sick of the whole business and especially of the long queue of craning necks that stretched from behind Mary to the door.

He bustled her off to wash her paws and then on to another room where they had to fill in a form with a lot of questions about Mary's parents and grand-parents and give details of other things about Mary such as how many infectious diseases she had had.

'Only measles,' said the Owl Man.

'And it tickled me,' added Mary.

Now, everyone going to America has to be vacci-nated, so Mary had been done two weeks before. At first she had been rather frightened, but directly she heard she could wear a red ribbon on her arm she was as brave as a lion. And though the arm did not 'take', she had worn the ribbon until that very morning. No red ribbon had ever been enjoyed more. 'I've been vacated!' she told everyone she met.

They visited several other desks. At one they had to produce the photographs they had had taken. 'There's four of me,' said Mary, handing them over rather reluctantly, and she was horrified when the man took some scissors and cut them in half.

At last they got to the final desk where a very im-portant official asked Mary to swear that all she had said was true.

'Whoopee! Yah! Bother!' said Mary promptly.

'Why, Mary!' exclaimed the Owl Man, while the

official looked at her over the top of his pince-nez and said, 'Is that all, young lady?'

'I'm afraid it's all the swear I know,' said Mary, regretfully.

'It'll do,' said the man, winking at the Owl Man. 'Well, I hope you have a very pleasant trip to the States, Miss – er –'

'Plain – Mary Plain. I'm an unusual first-class bear

from the bear-pits at Berne and I've got a white rosette and a gold medal with a picture of myself on it,' said Mary quickly and before the Owl Man could stop her.

'I'm awfully sorry,' he said.

'I'm not, I'm delighted,' said the official and he extended his hand to Mary with a 'Pleased to meet you, Miss Plain. You sure are unusual.'

Because Mary really had behaved very well under trying circumstances, the Owl Man bought her a whole bag of cream buns to eat in the car on their way to Harridges where there were still one or two last things they had to buy. They had a beautifully quiet drive as Mary did not speak once. She did not, however, waste a moment.

They went first to the ribbon counter to buy a blue ribbon for parties. The young assistant took a step backwards when she saw Mary, but when Mary made her second best bow she took one forward again.

Mary's head was just level with the counter and it was impossible for her to see, so the Owl Man lifted her on to the counter and the young lady produced a mirror so that Mary could see how terribly becoming the ribbons all were.

It was almost impossible to decide which to have.

'Aren't I beautiful!' exclaimed Mary, as the assistant exchanged a royal blue spot for a bird's-eye rayon.

Strangely enough, quite a lot of people seemed to be needing blue ribbon that morning and, by the time Mary had decided on a saxe blue satin, quite a Mary crowd had collected.

Unfortunately, the Owl Man asked, just a little too loudly, where raincoats were, so that the crowd suddenly changed their minds and realized it was raincoats and not ribbon they had wanted. The lift was so crowded that Mary nearly got trodden under-foot, and when she and the Owl Man and all the people got out at the second floor the raincoat assistants' hearts beat high in expectation of a huge sale.

The crowd, however, seemed to be in no hurry to be served and were far more interested in Mary's choice. Urged on by the Owl Man, who hated crowds as much as Mary loved them, she decided fairly quickly on a charming blue plastic with a hood, which fitted neatly into a small plastic envelope.

This time the Owl Man shook off the crowd very cleverly by waiting till the lift was nearly off and then nipping in with Mary at the last moment.

Their last visit was to the luggage department, for though Mary had a very gaily-striped zip-fastened bag which she always travelled with, the Owl Man felt she must have something quieter for the USA trip.

Mary pounced on a bright tartan suitcase, but the Owl Man said if she had that one, the beautiful picture label of the ship would not show up at all on it.

'This brown is sweetly pretty and would be very serviceable, Miss – Moddam – H'm,' said the assistant, who had never assisted a bear before and was a little uncertain how to address her.

Mary shook her head. 'It's the same colour as me and we might get mixed up.'

'How about this dainty blue, Miss – Moddam – H'm? It would make a good contrast to your coat – fur – skin – H'm,' and she held it against Mary's front.

'Blue is my best colour,' said Mary, uncertainly, 'but it's rather dark.'

'You really must decide, Mary, or we shall be late for our dinner – lunch – snack,' said the Owl Man, who found the assistant's trick catching. 'I should decide on the blue – brown – oh, hang!' he finished.

'Shall I tie up this fetching little confection then, Moddam – Mi –'

'Plain,' nipped in Mary. 'I'm Mary Pl –'

'Thank you,' interrupted the Owl Man, firmly, 'we'll take the blue. I'm in rather a hurry – have you any change?'

The girl handed him three pennies and he stuffed them into Mary's paw, seized it and the case and almost ran her down the stairs to the door.

It was nearly lunch-time and crowds of people were leaving for home or arriving for lunch.

'Follow me,' called the Owl Man.

Mary followed him in but she did not follow him out. She had never been in a revolving door before and she thought it wonderful. Round and round she went and she was so small that the people rushing in and out hid her from the Owl Man so he could not see where she was. At last he got a chance to grab her out.

'Really, Mary,' he said, giving her a little shake. 'What do you think you're doing?'

Mary ignored the shake. 'Wouldn't it be lovely to have a round-about door at the flat,' she said. 'Couldn't we, Owl Man? If I gave you back the three-pence?'

Three · Mary embarks on the *Englandic*

'HERE we go,' said the Owl Man, pushing Mary on to the gangway in front of him and congratulating himself on having had such an easy journey so far. By arriving early at Euston they had not only escaped the crowds but a little chat with the guard had secured them a carriage to themselves.

The Customs at Liverpool had been easy too, with only a slight delay when Mary insisted on declaring her gold medal. The officer had a look at it, but said he did not think she would get many dollars for that and let them go. And here they were – almost the first to board the beautiful big ship that lay shining and welcoming at the dock-side.

The eyebrows of the officer at the top of the gangway nearly went up into his hair when he saw Mary but, seeing his peaked cap, she gave him a very smart salute which he returned with equal smartness.

A few minutes later they were standing in cabin A49. It had two bunks, a big cupboard, an arm-chair and a chest; on the wall were brackets holding thermos jugs of water and glasses and, by the door, was the bathroom, complete with shower.

'Now, I'll just take my things out of my case,' said the Owl Man, 'and then you can unpack yours.'

Mary wandered round the room on an inspection tour. There was not much about but near their bunks were some fascinating buttons – a red, a green and a white one.

'What's that?' she inquired, pointing to a round white ball over the bunks, out of which came a soft roaring sound.

'It's air being pumped in,' said the Owl Man, 'and it's not – Come in.' The steward and stewardess did.

'Yes, sir?' said both, staring at Mary.

The Owl Man looked very surprised and then he looked at Mary. She had her back turned to him and, with her paws linked behind, she was kicking the carpet in a careless manner.

'Mary,' said the Owl Man, 'did you ring that bell?'

'I only pushed the button to see what would happen.'

'And we happened,' said the steward, good-humouredly.

'I'm so sorry,' said the Owl Man.

'That's all right, sir,' said the steward. 'Boys will be – I mean – h'm,' and he retired in confusion with the stewardess in fits of laughter.

'Now, Mary, please understand once and for all that no button or handle or knob that you may see in this ship is to be touched – ever. See?'

Mary saw. Her eyesight was awfully good at times.

The ship's engines were now throbbing and a series

of shouts and other noises meant that they were off. Mary sat on the ledge by the window and watched till England was a little speck in the distance.

'What's that?' she asked, as three short blasts sounded on the ship's horn.

'Boat drill,' said the Owl Man, lifting their safety-jackets off the wall and putting his on. 'Slip into this, Mary.'

But though Mary was only too ready to slip, she and the jacket did not seem to fit each other. Finally, the Owl Man carried it up to the boat station and there slid it over Mary's head. She was completely swamped.

'Are you there?' asked Mary at once, being unable to see anything but jacket. When he said he was she said, 'When does the marching drill begin?'

Several people turned and looked with startled eyes as they saw what appeared to be a furry-legged safety-jacket with an invisible voice.

The Owl Man, rather hot, bent down and explained it was not that kind of drill but a safety kind. When he unbent he saw that the boat-drillers were now all facing Mary instead of the sea.

'Are you still there?' asked Mary and when he again said 'Yes', she asked, 'What are we going to save?'

'Ourselves,' said the Owl Man, desperately and sweeping Mary and her jacket up under his arm he carried her back to the cabin and that was all the boat drill they did that day.

The Owl Man had arranged for Mary to have her supper in the cabin that first evening. He felt he really could not face the restaurant with Mary till the passengers were used to seeing her about.

When the gong sounded, Mary asked if she could go part of the way with him and the Owl Man said just to the end of the passage, and then Mary looked so wistfully at the stairs that, in the end, she went nearly to the dining-room door.

'Now cut along back, Mary,' said the Owl Man, and Mary cut.

She found No 49 quite easily. She was a little surprised to see a pink nylon night-dress laid out on her bunk, but how kind of the Owl Man to give her such a lovely surprise. Mary put it over her head. Oh, dear! it was far too big, but suddenly she felt so sleepy that nothing mattered but bed, so, holding the night-gown as high as possible, she dived under the clothes and in two ticks she was fast asleep.

So fast that she did not hear the cabin door open, some hours later, nor see a man and woman come in and switch on the light, nor even hear the shriek the woman gave as she saw Mary's head on the pillow. Her husband clapped his hand over her mouth. 'Shut up or you'll wake it,' he hissed and slowly and on tiptoe, with his hand still over her mouth in case another shriek came, he made her back to the door. Once outside he turned the key and they disappeared at a run.

A few moments later a procession arrived outside the cabin. Four stewards, carrying a large net, were pushed to the front.

'Go on! Hurry!' urged the ones behind, pushing.

'Here, stop shoving!' said one of the front ones, who kept licking his lips nervously. 'If you're Whipsnade trained, you'd better take on this job. I'm not.'

The pushing stopped at once.

'What is it, anyway?' asked someone.

No one seemed to know. When closely questioned, the displaced occupant murmured something about 'hairy and dangerous'.

'Humph!' said another, 'might be a fox!'

'Or a wolf.'

'Or a tiger.'

'Or even a lion,' added a hopeful voice from the very back.

The front steward swallowed. 'Come on, mates, let's get it over.' And gripping his corner of the net he opened the door and very stealthily and holding the net high, the four men crept up to the bunk, surrounded it and quickly dropped the net over it.

'Got it,' said one.

Mary, roused at last, sat up.

'Steady now, steady. Quiet, quiet,' said the largest

steward who held the corner nearest Mary's mouth. 'There, there,' he said, hoping to soothe.

But when she found she was shut in tight, Mary got in a panic and began struggling. 'Let me out! Let me out!' she shrieked.

Many helpful suggestions came from outside the cabin. 'Keep it down!' 'Knock it out!' 'Hit it on the head!'

Into this pandemonium strode the Owl Man. He had been hunting for Mary for over an hour and his relief at finding her was great even if it was in someone else's bunk. But when he had pushed his way to the front and saw the four men with the net and Mary's frantic efforts to get out, his eyes blazed. 'Let go that net,' he thundered, and with one pull he threw it on the floor.

Mary was trembling all over as she jumped into his arms and it took quite a few moments' stroking to calm her. Her would-be captors stood round looking rather foolish as they saw how quiet and un-fierce Mary really was.

'Why did they net me?' she asked in a shaky voice. 'I only went to bed.'

'But in the wrong bunk,' said the Owl Man, going on patting.

'But it had 49 on the door,' insisted Mary.

'Ninety-four,' corrected the Owl Man. 'You got it the wrong way round.'

Mary looked down at the pink nylon floating round the Owl Man's legs.

'Isn't this the right night-gown, either?' she asked.

'I'm afraid not,' said the Owl Man, 'but (watching Mary's ears) I'll get you another – a better fit.'

'Blue?'

'Blue,' said the Owl Man.

The ears were now in points.

Four · Mary attends a fancy-dress dinner with her usual success

AFTER the episode of Mary getting into the wrong bunk, all hope of keeping her in the background had to be abandoned. She became the most popular person on board. Young men gave her flowers, old men kissed her paw and ladies of every age begged for her autograph.

After a day of this the Owl Man put his foot down and a notice up.

RE THE CUB, MARY PLAIN
To whom it may concern

Please note that unless above cub can be left in quiet, receiving no kindly-meant attentions of any sort, her owner will regretfully be obliged to keep her in strict privacy.

For a day after that everyone that saw Mary looked the other way or turned round and walked in the opposite direction.

Mary was appalled. 'Why do they all disappear?' she asked the Owl Man. 'Don't they like me any more?'

The Owl Man said there was such a thing as liking someone too much, but Mary shook her head. 'Not me,' she said.

Things, however, righted themselves and by the third day Mary was happily pursuing her own way, which seemed to lead to every corner of the ship. She turned up in the most unexpected places – on the Captain's bridge, in the Chief Purser's private cabin and in the engine room and in the Tourist Class.

She had to be rescued from there, for the tourists did not know about her and her appearance caused a stampede which was only stopped when a steward shut her neatly into a pantry and locked the door.

Luckily, he reported direct to the Captain. 'Unidentified wild animal wandering at large in the Tourist Section, now safely confined to pantry' was how he put it, and when the Captain asked, 'Are you referring to a small bear cub, Laurence?' he got rather pink and stammered, 'Ye – yes, sir.'

He was astounded when the Captain hurried back with him in person to release Mary. She accepted his apologies gracefully – also a box of chocolates which he produced, like a conjuror, out of his pocket.

The days flew by and the last evening came, on which there was to be a fancy-dress gala dinner.

Mary refused to tell anyone, even the Owl Man, what she was going to wear. That morning, she had asked for a week's pocket-money in advance and had spent the whole sixpence on a box of safety-pins at the ship's shop.

From tea-time onwards she locked herself into the bathroom and refused to answer any questions or to come out. The wretched Owl Man had to go and have his bath down the corridor without a sponge.

In the restaurant the waiters had had a busy afternoon. Some of the flowers that people had sent to the ship were still beautifully fresh, but some were less lucky and for every table which had none, the head dining-room steward had arranged a small vase of red button chrysanthemums which they had in store.

It all looked very gay and festive when the staff went off to their late tea, feeling very pleased with themselves.

It was at six-thirty, half an hour before dinner-time, that the head steward, going back again to have a final look round, gave a cry that brought all the other waiters at a run.

'Oh!' and 'OOh!' they moaned, as well they might. For a dreadful thing had happened. During their hour away someone had been in and removed the flowers from several tables. The button chrysanthemums had not been touched – it was the guest's various private flowers that had been removed and the table-cloths splashed with water from their stems.

The head waiter could have said a lot but all he did say was 'Quick! Clean table-cloths for fourteen tables and there's some more chrysants in the store-room. Everybody get going!'

Meantime, the Owl Man and Mary were having a heated argument through the bathroom door. The Owl Man, feeling uncomfortably hot in his own Burberry, the Chief Engineer's sea-boots and the deck-steward's souwester as 'English Weather', was trying, without any success, to get Mary out. In the end, he had to go to dinner alone and sat down with an anxious eye on the door.

He did not have long to wait. About half-way through the 'Lobster Newburg' there were loud exclamations from people sitting near the door. The band-leader turned his head and quickly changed the tune to a roll on the drum and on the roll Mary made her entrance.

Just inside the door she stopped and made three bows, one to the right, one to the left and one to the centre – rather stiff bows as her head-dress was apt to wobble, but they brought terrific applause.

The Owl Man had to confess she had not done too badly. She had tied two bunchy towels round her middle, a fair imitation of a ballet-skirt, and on to this was pinned a kind of garden border.

Freesias, pansies and anemones rampaged over the

skirt while a sash of plaited ferns hid the string round her middle – necklaces of daffodils dangled gaily from her neck, while in her arms she carried a large basket full of small bunches of the flowers she had not been able to find room for. She was crowned with a cardboard circle on which was printed in huge capitals 'MARY PLAIN. FLOUR GIRL'.

When she turned her head, the Owl Man could see that something was written on the back but he was too far off to see what it was. Though they were standing on their chairs the people farthest off could not see Mary and there were cries of 'Come over here and show yourself'.

More than willingly, Mary started on a solo grand parade of the restaurant. During her progress she overheard many stifled exclamations of 'My freesias!' 'My gardenias!' 'My carnation!' of which she took not the slightest notice. Every now and then she threw a few flowers to right and left. 'Well fielded!' whispered one husband as his wife caught one of her own orchids.

Back at the door, the Owl Man was waiting for Mary. Cries of 'Speech!' 'Speech!' were now started and, as Mary turned her head, he saw what was written on the back. He got very red and whispered sternly, 'Keep facing the room, Mary, for Pete's sake!'

The cries were now so loud that something had to

be done about it and the Captain did it. He removed the vase of flowers from his table and replaced it with Mary. She whispered something and the Captain clapped his hands.

'Pray silence for Miss Mary Plain,' he said and, to everyone but the Owl Man's surprise, Mary burst into song. He had been teaching her one or two American songs and, as usual, she chose a well-known one and fitted her own words to it. This time it was 'Polly-Wolly Doodle'.

> For I'm crossing the Atlantic
> In the ship that's called *Englandic*,
> Singing Mary Plain O'Doodle all the way.
> Tomorrow comes New York
> And away we all shall walk
> Singing Mary Plain O'Doodle all the way.
>
> Fare thee well,
> Fare thee well,
> Fare thee well, to all I say,
> Mary Plain is going Usa,
> And you'll soon be going to lose her.
> Singing Mary Plain O'Doodle all the way.
>
> I'll say 'Thank you' to the crew
> And to every one of you,
> Singing Mary Plain O'Doodle all the way,

And you know I won't forget you
And you'll think of me, I bet you,
Singing Mary Plain O'Doodle all the way.

Fare thee well,
Fare thee well,
Fare thee well to all I say,
Mary Plain is going to Usa,
And you'll soon be going to lose her,
Singing Mary Plain O'Doodle all the way.

Thunderous applause followed and Mary, bowing and waving to the people, now all massed round the Captain's table, threw the remaining flowers from her basket. The Captain stood up on his chair and once more asked for silence.

'I think everyone will want me to say a very big "Thank you" to Miss Plain for her apt and charming song.' (Tremendous clapping and cries of 'Hear! Hear!') 'And I'm sure you'll also agree that her delightful costume merits the first prize.' (Deafening cheers.)

Mary looked across at the Owl Man and deliberately winked. Then she took off her head-dress and turned it carefully back to front.

On it was written, rather larger than life,

MISS PLAIN. 1st PRIZE

Five · In which Mary startles New York

'WAIT a second, Mary, while I collect a red-cap,' said the Owl Man and he ran to a porter standing near.

Mary did not want to move. She was gazing with great interest at the high roof – her head well back. A woman passed between her and the pile of luggage.

'Where are the bees, please?' asked Mary.

The woman slipped behind the luggage before she answered, 'Bees? There aren't any bees here.'

'But I can hear them,' insisted Mary.

The woman moved away quickly. Was she dreaming or was it true that a live bear had asked her, right here on the docks in 51st Street, about bees? Looking back she saw that a tall man in spectacles had joined Mary and was laughing.

'That's the hum of New York,' he was saying, 'not bees . . .'

'Then I like New York,' said Mary. 'It makes me think of honey.' The drive to the hotel in a yellow taxi was exciting. There were masses of huge, brightly coloured cars dashing about and just not hitting each other.

'Haven't the houses grown tall!' said Mary. 'I can only see a little bit of sky.'

'They're called sky-scrapers,' said the Owl Man, 'and some of them have over eighty stories.'

'What are the stories about – bears?'

'Not that kind, floors, landings, I meant. Here we are. Now, take your case, Mary, and get out.'

The manager was there to receive them in person, partly because the Owl Man was an old client but more because Mary was the first bear he had ever had as a guest.

The Owl Man shook hands and then introduced

Mary. The manager shook Mary's paw warmly and said, 'This is a great pleasure, Miss Plain.'

'Hi!' said Mary, which was the only American she had yet learned.

'Listen to that!' said the manager. 'Isn't she cute?'

'In my fur suit,' said Mary, smartly. Too smartly, thought the Owl Man as he hurried her into the lift.

They shot up ten floors and were shown into two communicating rooms with a bathroom in between.

'This is fine,' said the Owl Man.

'You're welcome,' said the manager, as he went off.

Lunch was a new experience for Mary. She sipped a Coca-Cola and watched the coloured waiters flying round with huge trays laden with food. The Owl Man had a rare beefsteak but for Mary he ordered a pile of buck-wheat cakes and hot maple syrup. Mary liked the syrup a little better than the buckwheat, so the jug had to be refilled three times. She was so hungry that she never asked a single question till the pile had gone and then she said, 'Pudding, please.'

'Are you quite sure, Mary?' asked the Owl Man.

Mary nodded. 'One of those, please,' she said, pointing to a huge ice-cream soda the waiter was carrying past.

She disposed of the last atom of ice-cream and then said she'd like another, but the Owl Man said there was no time as he had to hurry off to an appointment at once.

Mary went, too. Mostly because, though she was not altogether a convenient person to take to a business talk, she would probably be even more inconvenient if left behind. Actually, it turned out very well. There were two charming young secretaries in the office who were quite ready to look after her.

They asked Mary if she had flown over. 'I flowned once,' said Mary, 'but this time we came in a ship and I won first prize.'

'You don't say!' said the girls. 'Do tell us.' So Mary told and left nothing out. She even sang her song to them.

After that they let her do a bit of typing, but Mary's paws made the letters come out in words like this – qwer-sdfg-cvbnm-asdfg, which were too difficult to read.

'Let's send her down the shoot,' suggested the prettiest girl. 'Would you care to go, Miss Plain?'

'Please,' said Mary, who was ready to go down anything once.

The shoot was in the wall and it was made of polished wood. It started in the office and ended in a packing room two floors below and a lot of parcels were sent down every day.

One of the girls opened the door and called, 'Hi! you below there. There's a special kind of parcel coming down – a darling one. Will one of you escort it back up the stairs, please?'

The 'darling parcel' shot down like a streak of lightning and, because the shoot had an upward bend at the bottom it arrived on its back. While Mary got herself right side up a complete silence reigned. The silence was made by six girls in a row – all staring.

'Wal,' said one. 'Guess you're very welcome,' and she held out her hand.

'Pleased to meet you,' said Mary, who was picking up American like anything.

'Have some toffee?' offered one.

Mary had lots, and they all chatted happily.

Then one of the girls offered to take her upstairs, but Mary said she knew the way and would like to go alone, please. So they watched her start off up the stairs, but the moment the door was closed Mary turned round and galloped down again 'on an explore', as she called it.

It was a long way down, but at last Mary emerged in 7th Avenue. She stood and looked across the wide street and seeing a window with lots of sweets labelled 'CANDY FOR YOU!' she decided to go across and get some, but, as she moved, a woman saw her and shrieked and in a moment there were men shouting, children screaming, and before you could say Jack Robinson a clear space was left round her. She still stood quietly in the doorway. The people behind who could not see Mary, hearing murmurs of 'wild animal' and 'escape from Zoo', etc., began calling for the police.

Most fortunately, the Owl Man who, back in the office, had quickly discovered Mary was missing, dashed down in the lift and arrived at the door just in time, to find a seething Mary crowd out of which, at a

crouch, approached six policemen with pistols lev-
elled, while two more halted the traffic in each direction.

If he had not been so annoyed at the publicity (why
did Mary always choose places like 7th Avenue to
create scenes?) the Owl Man could have laughed at
the sight of six armed police, backed by a huge crowd,
facing one small cub! As it was, he pushed Mary
behind him and explained to the nearest officer that
no firearms were necessary – that the cub was his and
perfectly harmless.

Slowly the police lowered their pistols and, standing
in a circle, surveyed Mary. At close quarters she certainly seemed quite harmless.

'Has she a passport?' asked one, suspiciously.

The Owl Man at once produced it – and his own.

'Looks all in order,' said the policeman, scratching
his head. 'But a bear in 7th Avenue don't happen
every day of the week.'

'Sure,' said a second. 'It kinda took us by surprise.'

'She's kinda cute,' said a third. 'What do you call
her?'

Here Mary took over. First she bowed a bear bow
which, as we all know, means bending down and looking backwards through your legs. Then she said, 'I'm
an unusual first-class bear from the bear-pits at Berne
and I've got a white rosette and a gold medal with a

picture of myself on it and please can I go over to that shop called "Candy" because I'm hungry.'

By this time, all the traffic between 29th and 78th Street, was in a solid jam and all the cars, taxis and buses were hooting their horns like mad. But, before they were released, a little procession crossed over. Mary, perched on the Owl Man's shoulder, was surrounded by a little posse of police, all with their pistols re-holstered.

'Many thanks,' said the Owl Man, on the opposite side-walk.

'Good luck! See you again. Enjoy the candy!' called the police. 'Glad to know you!'

'Hi!' shouted Mary as loud as she could, but her voice was drowned in the renewed roar of the traffic.

Six · Mary pays a country s'visit

THE Owl Man and Mary in a 'drive yourself' car were on their way down to the country for a day's visit or s'visit, as Mary always called it, to some friends of his who had two little girls. The drive was lovely. The wide freeway was as smooth as marble and the trees on each side had on their bright 'fall' frocks. The sign-posting, as always in the States, was excellent and only when they got to the small town outside which the friends lived, did they have to ask a man the way.

'Way down at the bottom of the street,' he said. 'About two blocks off. You'll see the name on the letterbox at the gate.'

They did, indeed, and also saw Missy and Rosa-mund standing by it and waving hard.

Their Mummy and Daddy ran down to the gate and everyone seemed delighted to see everyone else and, while the grown-ups were talking, the children took Mary up to the house and down to their play-room where they had some wonderful toys. When

they were tired of playing, they sat down and Mary told them all about how she won her medal and then it was time for lunch.

There, for the first time, Mary was introduced to corn on the cob. She ate three whole cobs and got so drowned in butter that she had to be removed to the bathroom and have what was practically a shampoo. And after came waffles and maple syrup and soon Mary was in a worse state than before.

'I don't seem to have made a very wise choice of food,' said the Mummy, as she led Mary off for the second time, but Mary's tongue was so busy that she was almost clean by the time they got upstairs.

After lunch the Daddy took the Owl Man to call on his parents while the others went down to the Community Centre to do some shopping. The Mummy parked the car and said she was just going to slip along to collect a book from a friend and would be back in a few moments. But it turned out to be a good many moments and the children and Mary got bored waiting in the hot car.

'I go to school now,' said Rosamund rather grandly, 'and I can write MAT and it means mat.'

'I have my own special writing,' said Mary, in a superior voice.

'Oh, do show us,' begged the children, searching in the car pocket for a pencil and paper.

So Mary wrote.

⬛M AN UNUSUAL 🐻 FROM THE BEAR-PITS

N ⬭ BERNE N 🖐 IVE GOT A WHITE 🌹

AND A GOLD 🏅 WITH A 📷 OF MYSELF

ON IT.

Both children were delighted.
'Is it true?' asked Missy.
'Of course,' said Mary. 'This is, too.' And she
wrote.

I'M THIRSTY 🫖 I HAVE
A 🥤 PLEZE

It was Missy's turn to say 'Of course,' because she
was Mary's hostess. She looked in her purse and found
she had eighty cents. 'Let's go over to the Automat,'
she suggested.

When Mary got inside and saw the row of taps
labelled 'Chocolate', 'Tea', 'Coffee', 'Orange Juice',
'Grape Fruit Juice', her eyes popped with excitement. 'You put your nickel in here, I'll show you,'
explained Missy, and she put one in the Grape Fruit

and one in the Orange for herself and Rosamund. 'Now you try!' and she held out her hand with sixty cents in it.

'Oh, thank you,' said Mary, taking the lot. Beginning at the chocolate, she worked her way along the row, while the two children followed behind uttering little exclamations of admiration as the coffee, milk, tea and fruit juices followed each other down Mary's throat.

'Which did you like best?' inquired Rosamund, at the end.

'All,' said Mary, licking her lips.

Next they wandered into the Community Store two doors off and Mary's eyes popped more than ever as she saw the long counters piled with everything you could possibly want.

'What kind of a shop is it?' she asked.

'It's a kind of "help yourself" store,' explained Missy. 'You take what you want and they wrap it for you on your way out. See, we take one of these little trollies to collect the things in,' and she pushed a kind of wire basket on wheels towards Mary. 'Like to take it?'

'I'd rather ride,' said Mary. 'I could see better.'

So she hopped in and the girls pushed her down the first aisle, but their progress was slow as at each counter Mary saw something she wanted and shouted 'Stop!'

By the time they reached the bottom of the store, Mary had collected so many things that she was almost pushed out of the basket herself.

'I'll sit on top,' she said, 'then I can see better.'

So she got out while the boxes of candy and cartons of biscuits, the cakes and toys and bananas were all piled up in the trolly and then, with the children's help, Mary perched herself on the rather wobbly pile.

There really was no room for anything more, so Mary, who still kept on crying 'Stop!' had to wear the rest of the things. When at last they reached the exit door you could hardly see her at all.

She had one arm through a bright red rain-coat and the other through a brilliantly striped duffle coat. Huge rubber boots were on her hind paws, several pearl necklaces round her neck, sun-glasses hid her eyes, while on top was balanced a large raffia hat in every colour of the rainbow.

The man at the wrapping counter looked very startled as this extraordinary group pulled up beside him. He had had no idea that they sold wild animals at the store, as this was his first day there. He hoped it had no grizzly blood because his uncle had known a man who was hugged to death by one.

One thing had been drilled into him. He must let nothing leave the store unless it was properly wrapped. So, when Missy suggested that he enter the

things to her mother's account and allow them to take the things through to the car and unpack it there, he shook his head.

'I'm sorry,' he said, 'but every purchase has to be wrapped right here.'

Making a secret vow that he would transfer the very next day to a piano store where there would be nothing to wrap, he said, in a voice which only shook a little, 'We'll begin at the top.' He helped Mary down on to the counter but before he could wrap her he had to unwrap all her purchases. This done, he dived under his counter and came up with a huge paper bag.

'But you can't wrap her – she's alive,' cried Missy, appalled.

'Rules is rules, no purchase, whatsoever, is to leave this store unwrapped,' answered the man.

'But she isn't a purchase – she's a bear!' said Missy.

'Isn't that just too bad,' said the man. 'Now, in you go!' and he popped the paper bag over Mary's head.

The head immediately popped out at the other end. When three bags had been burst, the man started with her feet. But though the bag slid easily up to her middle, there it stuck and above there was just unwrapped bear.

The man ran his hand distractedly through his

hair. 'I've got it!' he exclaimed suddenly, and rushed away down the centre aisle.

He returned waving a long white cellophane dress bag. It was so long that the only way he could get Mary in was to lie her flat on the counter. They had just got her zipped up when the Mummy and Daddy and the Owl Man came rushing in.

Mary, almost afraid to breathe in case she split the bag, was lying like a stone and when the Owl Man saw the still white form he turned very pale. 'Is she – dead?' he gasped out and he nearly burst with relief when a voice from the bag said, 'No – only wrapped. But, please, please, Owl Man, unzip me quickly.'

The next moment Mary, her head very ruffled, was out of the bag and gazing reproachfully at the assembled company.

'They don't wrap bears in England,' she said.

Seven · Which is full of para-pets, parades and police

MARY was bored, and too hot, too.

The Owl Man went out directly after lunch and, though he had left Mary some copies of children's papers to look at, she had finished them very quickly.

Wandering over to the writing-table, she opened the drawer and found some sheets of writing paper with a picture of the hotel on each. This was better. Mary hunted about and found a pencil and soon there was a picture of Mary under every one of the hotel. Drawing them filled up one of the spaces between the bellboy's visit.

The bellboy had got a whole dollar in his pocket on the understanding that he would put his head in through the door (which he was to keep locked on the outside) every half-hour – just to make sure Mary was all right.

So, just as Mary was finishing the last picture, his head popped round the door.

'Everything hunky-dory?' he inquired.

'I'm too hot,' complained Mary. 'Do, please, open the window.'

Under the window was a notice which said 'This room is air-conditioned. Please do not open the window.'

The bellboy hesitated and then looked at Mary, panting a little in her fur coat, and decided it really was cruelty to be shut up on a day like this, so he opened it from the bottom.

'Oh, thank you,' said Mary, gratefully.

'O.K.,' said the boy as he went off.

Outside the window was a kind of low parapet that ran along past the window. Mary leaned out, and way below she could just see the traffic on 5th Avenue – tiny toy cars and buses and wee little people hurrying past.

Suddenly, a siren wailed, louder and louder, and

along came a fire-engine, two fire-engines – no three! counted Mary, excitedly, leaning as far out as she could get. But it was not quite far enough to see comfortably and the parapet looked most inviting. So out she climbed and sat on it, drumming her heels and watching the street several hundred feet below. Soon after the fire-engines came another siren and this time it was an ambulance and then after a bit came a quite new noise and Mary pricked her ears. What could it be? It was not the usual hum and it sounded like music.

Yes, it was music! It was a band and here it came, heading a long procession. Mary's paws drummed like anything. She adored processions and she watched with increasing interest the marching people who looked like a big snake winding its way along the Avenue.

But it was really all too far off and Mary began to wish she was down below. Looking along the parapet, she could see that, at the end of the building, it seemed to go round the corner. Very carefully on all fours, she crept along it. Yes, it did turn and oh! hurrah! in the narrow space between this building and the next block was a narrow steel stair-case. Perhaps those stairs had never been descended with such speed before and in only four minutes Mary was down in the street.

Everybody was so absorbed in watching the procession that she was able to slip right up to the edge of the crowd and get a close-up view. How lovely the people looked! Some wore uniforms and some wore capes and some wore top-hats and wide sashes across their chests and most of them seemed to be carrying a 'Stars and Stripes' flag.

And what wonderful music! Mary's paws began to mark time.

Here came a group of children – all dressed in white frocks with bright-coloured bands round the skirts and, in front, one of them marched proudly alone, tossing up a red and blue striped baton and catching it again – most cleverly.

Mary could resist it no longer. The music said 'Come' and she went.

She slipped alongside the marching children and because they were so well trained, only their eyes swerved to the right and took Mary in and if they stayed right who was to blame them, so long as they kept on marching?

No one did anything about Mary because she was marching so beautifully in time with her head up and her front out and her presence only caused extra clapping as she passed. Every time the procession was halted to let the traffic across, Mary managed to slip one place farther in and presently she was in the very middle of the marching children – in the front row, of course.

Somehow, she got hold of a flag and soon after that she was just a few paces ahead of the line and immediately behind the drum-major. More than that Mary could not hope for, for she knew she could not throw that stick about without dropping it – not without a lot of practice.

All went well till the band struck up 'My country, 'tis of thee', which has the same tune as 'God save the Queen'.

Mary stopped dead and bringing her paw up in a stiff salute, she remained immovable in the middle of the Avenue while all the small girls in their national costumes jammed up behind her.

By the greatest good fortune, the Owl Man was walking back to the hotel along 5th Avenue and, when this jamming up of the marchers took place, he pushed his way through the crowd to see what had happened.

'Great Christopher Columbus!' he exclaimed, blinking hard to see if he was imagining things. But when he stopped blinking, Mary was still there, stiff as a ramrod while the unsuspecting band went on playing the tune that kept her there.

The Owl Man saw in a minute what had happened. He dashed to the nearest official and explained rapidly about standing to attention when 'God save the Queen' was played and the official dashed to the band-leader, who quickly changed the tune to 'Hail Columbia', and Mary came out of her salute and started off again.

The Owl Man, wishing very much that Mary would not choose such public places for these appearances, ran out to her side and tried to stop her but the music and the marching had gone to Mary's head and on she went, keeping beautiful time and loving every step. And the Owl Man found himself in the ridiculous position of marching down 5th Avenue in company with a bear and in step with a battalion of small children in national costumes all waving 'Stars and Stripes'. He had never felt so British in his life and the next time the traffic lights stopped them, and Mary was off her guard, he swooped her up under his arm and carried her, kicking furiously, to the side-walk.

There he put her down and gave her a little shake and a woman passing said she would report him to the police authorities if he did it again.

Somehow, he got Mary down a side-street and found a taxi to take them back to their hotel. Back in their rooms he looked at her in despair. 'How did you get out, Mary?'

'It was hot, so I sat on the wall and then I crawled along it and found a staircase. The band was calling me,' she added.

The Owl Man looked out of the open window and shuddered. Mary looked out too and wished very much she was down below, still marching.

'Next birthday, please, I'd like a stick with red and blue stripes on it,' she said.

Eight · Mary boards the west-bound Zephyr

MARY and the Owl Man travelled over-night to Chicago and joined the Californian Zephyr next day. It was the most exciting train that Mary had ever seen – all gleaming silver and so long you could not see the engine. The big coaches all had silvery names too, like 'Silver Creek', 'Silver Swallow' and the one they were in was called 'Silver Arrow'.

Outside their coach, the coloured attendant was talking to his wife who had brought their little boy to say 'Good-bye'. He was black as coal with tight curls and an engaging grin.

'Is that your piccaninny?' asked the Owl Man.

'Sure,' said the father, with a very white-toothed smile.

'What's he picking?' inquired Mary and the father laughed and said piccaninny was just a name for a baby and this one was really too big for it – he was getting to be quite a boy.

The Owl Man and Mary had a nice, cosy compartment. He had bought some sandwiches in Chicago so they had a private picnic dinner and Mary was waiter and served the sandwiches with a napkin over her paw.

'Ham or egg, Owl Man, sir?' she inquired, and when he had chosen ham she said, 'Ham or egg, Miss Plain, madam?'

'Both, please,' said Miss Plain, helping herself.

It was fun and afterwards Mary had a rather too splashy wash in the little toilet and they went to bed so as to be up bright and early in the Vista-dome next morning.

It was a beautiful day and they were the first people up there. The Vista-dome is a room up on the roof of the train with big windows all round so you have a wonderful view of the country-side. The Owl Man chose the front seats so that no one would have to pass them.

It was an exciting run; they crawled up mountains and down mountains and shot into tunnels and over rivers and always there was something interesting to see. Once or twice, the Owl Man wondered why nobody came up. It was extraordinary that people should miss a chance like this.

Later on, he slipped down for some cigarettes and was astonished to find the passage below completely blocked with people, all looking longingly up above.

'There are plenty of seats,' he said.

'Is IT up there?' asked a fat woman in front.

'It?' repeated the Owl Man and then he suddenly realized what she meant. 'If you mean my tame, kind little bear – it is.'

'Truly?' said the woman. 'It won't bite, or hug or anything?'

'Mary!' called the Owl Man and Mary appeared at the top of the stairs. 'Will you act attendant and show these people to their seats?'

'Please step up,' said Mary, importantly.

No one moved for a moment and then there was an upward rush.

When the Owl Man got back there was only one seat left, so Mary had to sit on his knee. Suddenly a voice spoke. 'Attention, please! This is your Zephyrette speaking.'

Mary looked everywhere and then she got down and looked under the seat.

'Have you dropped something, Mary?' asked the Owl Man.

'I'm looking for the voice,' said Mary, 'and why can it talk?'

Laughter greeted this remark and the Owl Man had to say, 'Sh!' very loudly, for the poor Zephyrette could not be heard. While he explained in a whisper to Mary where the voice was coming from, the Zephyrette told them they would shortly be going through the Glenwood Canyon, which was one of the most beautiful canyons in the world, and, till then, there would be some light music for their entertainment. Almost at once a voice began singing, 'Way down upon the Swanee river'. This was one of the songs the Owl Man had been teaching Mary and she began to sing her own words to the music. The wireless was tuned very low, so Mary's voice could easily be heard above it.

This was her song:

Down in the Californian Zephyr,
Here we all go
It's such a lovely train, I neffer
Saw such a lovely train before.
Now, that together we are roaming,
Mary Plain and you,
Together we are Vista-doming,
Mary Plain and everyone and you.

All the way I keep on singing
Mary Plain and me,
How lucky that we're all beginning
A silver Zephyr trip to the sea.

The song was such a success that the Owl Man hurried Mary off to lunch before anyone could suggest an encore. They had it in a small snack-bar just below where chicken or fish salads and sandwiches were served quickly so that you could hurry back to the Vista-dome and the view.

But the Owl Man thought he would have a little rest before he returned. Travelling with Mary was never exactly peaceful, so they went back to their coach and he slipped into the carriage adjoining theirs to have a chat with another man.

It was very hot in the train and often, when they halted at the small stations, Mary and the Owl Man would get out for a breath of fresh air.

On this afternoon, at one of these halts, the Zephyr had a shower. Some kind of engine above shot gallons of water on to the roof which poured down the sides, cleaning the dust and dirt off the windows on its way.

Lucky Zephyr! thought Mary, her nose pressed against the glass. How beautifully cool it looked and how terribly hot the carriage was. She peeped into the next compartment, but the Owl Man seemed very interested in his talk and showed no sign of moving, so Mary decided to slip out by herself.

There were quite a few people on the platform and, for once, Mary did not want to be seen, so she immediately slipped between two coaches and crawled through to the farther side of the train. Before she emerged, however, she lay for a moment under the water pouring down and got soaked all over. It was

deliciously refreshing and when she came out she
looked just like a drowned rat with her fur flat and
shiny.

This platform was empty. Mary looked up and
down the train and wondered if the back had had a
shower, too. Or the front, perhaps?

The water seemed to be stopping now, but she decided just to slip along and see if the engine was nice
and clean. She had better hurry, though, as it would
soon be time to leave.

Mary started galloping and yet, fast as she went,
she never seemed to catch the engine and it was only
when she had reached the end of the platform that she
realized she was not catching it because the train was
on the move.

'HI!' yelled Mary. 'Stop! Stop! I'm left behind.
Stop!'

But her voice was drowned by the train's hooter as it approached a road crossing. And everyone was looking out of the farther side of the train, so nobody saw the little figure frantically waving. Faster, faster came the coaches and now the last one rushed past her.

'Stop! Oh, please do stop!' yelled Mary, galloping down the track behind the Zephyr, which gathered speed every moment. It disappeared round a bend, but Mary, her breath coming in little sobbing pants, still galloped on.

Perhaps there would be another station round the next corner or perhaps it would stop to have another bath and she could catch it up. But round the bend there was still no sign of the Zephyr and, at last, because she really had no breath left, Mary pulled up.

At first she could only hear her own pants but presently there came a soft roaring kind of noise. A hooter sounded and she turned, caught her paw and fell flat. There was a shout and a harsh screaming of brakes as a break-down van pulled up just a yard short of her.

Down from it jumped two men to get a close-up view of what had caused a near accident. Mary looked so small and forlorn lying there, looking up at them from under her long lashes, that they picked her up and carried her to their van and there, directly she got her breath back, Mary told them what had happened.

'Could you, please, catch the Zephyr for me?' she begged, earnestly.

Catching the Zephyr was not really the business of the van, but Mary's voice had a little shake in it and the driver stuck his chin out as far as it would go and said he'd do his darndest.

And so the chase began.

Nine · In which Mary chases the Zephyr

THE driver wedged Mary into the seat between him and the engineer. 'Hold tight!' he said, grimly.

The truck, which had been built to move workmen up and down the 2,500 mile track, wherever they were needed, and not to catch Zephyrs, was soon rushing along at a terrific pace.

They whizzed round bends and up and down mountains, shot in and out of tunnels and dashed across bridges, and all the time Mary felt perfectly certain the Zephyr would be waiting for them round the next corner but it never was. They went at such a pace that Mary's ears blew up in points and the men had to fasten the chin-straps on their caps.

When they got on to a fairly straight bit of track the engineer handed Mary some chewing-gum. What happened they could not tell, but the next moment Mary was choking badly. The man patted her hard on the back and made her put her head right down, but it was no good. Bears cannot go black in the face so Mary stayed brown, but it was evident that the chewing-gum really had got stuck, for she could not get her breath.

'Have to stop,' said the engineer.

'Can't!' said the driver. 'But I'll slow up a bit and you can hang her over the edge upside down and give her a shake.' Which he did. Poor Mary, held by her back paws, saw Colorado upside down, but it did the trick, for when she saw it right side up again the gum had gone.

Once Mary had got her breath back she began to be sorry she had wasted the gum. 'Could I have another, please?' she asked.

'Not on your life!' said the driver.

Mary sighed. 'Could I drive the engine, then? I drove a big ship once.'

'Maybe,' said the driver, 'but you'll not be driving this truck, young lady. I thought you wanted bad to catch that Zephyr?'

'Oh, I do!' said Mary, 'but we never seem to, do we?'

Just then they pulled up at a way-side station for just long enough to ask how long it was since the Zephyr had left.

'Twenty minutes!' called the man in charge.

The driver scowled and squared his already square chin and off they went, faster, even, than before.

At the next stop they heard they were only ten minutes behind.

'We'll do it yet!' said the driver, between his teeth. We're nearly at the place where the two Zephyrs cross, and ours will have to draw on to the side-track to let the Eastern-bound one pass. That will be our chance. If only we can make it. We sure must!'

Whizz went the trees and swish went the river and phht went the telegraph poles as they shot past them. 'Ten miles more – five – three – one,' ticked off the driver.

'I can hear the horn of the up-coming train,' said the engineer. Down went the throttle. Quicker! Faster! And now they were almost flying. One more bridge. Swish! they were over. One more corner. Whoops! they were round and there, calmly shining in the sun, lay the great silver train.

The driver slowed down to a crawl and pulled Mary between his knees. 'Now, you can drive her in,' he said. So Mary, proud as a peacock, held the wheel till they slowed to a standstill behind their Zephyr just as her incoming sister swung into view.

But what was this? The eastern-bound Zephyr never stopped here but it was slowing up this time and now it was just crawling.

'Well, I'll be darned!' said the driver. 'I've never seen that happen before. Why, say! There's a guy in spectacles climbing down from our Zephyr. He's on the track now and yes! he's going to – hi! young lady, what's wrong?'

'Quick! Quick! It's the Owl Man, oh, quick!' yelled Mary, wriggling frantically to free herself. The next instant she was down on the ground and racing along the side of the track towards the eastern-bound train.

Mary was quite right – it was the Owl Man. The train had slowed down just enough to let him swing himself on board. The truck-driver began to sound his horn hard and all the people in the observation car at the back of the western Zephyr looked out to see what was happening, and directly they saw Mary they all got highly excited and rushed away to tell the attendants.

In a matter of seconds the Zephyr's horn was also hooting like mad and the Owl Man turned his head to see what was causing such a hullabaloo and saw the cause just below him, dancing up and down in a frenzy and waving both arms.

The train had now gathered some speed but, without stopping to think, the Owl Man took a flying leap and landed beside Mary on all fours. The porters flung their luggage after them and a huge cheer went up.

Mary was explaining as fast as she could about the kind van-men who had rescued her, but the Owl Man had no time to run along and thank them, for all the officials on the Californian Zephyr were shouting to ask them if they wanted to be left behind.

'Help!' said the Owl Man, seizing Mary and throwing her to their attendant, who made a very clever catch. He then bundled himself and their cases aboard, and they were off.

So Mary sent a wire to the truck-driver from the next stop which said, 'Thank you for catching the Zephyr for me and a big Hi from yours sincerely Mary Plain.' And the driver had it framed, and hung it in his parlour for it is not everyone that possesses a personal telegram from a real live bear.

In the Zephyr, a tremendous fuss was made of Mary. Everyone wanted to treat her to Coca-Cola and the Zephyrette had a special good-bye tea served for them at her table.

Despite the Coca-Colas, Mary was so thirsty after her gallop that she drank five cups of tea before she began to eat, but it did not seem to affect her appetite in the least and, in the end and as usual, the Owl Man had to put his foot down.

'And I have to run along,' said the hostess. 'We're only a short way from San Francisco and I have to give a farewell message to our travellers.'

'May I come, too?' inquired Mary, eagerly.

'Sure!' said the Zephyrette. 'You can stand by and give me your support.'

And of course, Mary's support was very charac-

teristic. When the Zephyrette's voice ended, a buzz of low-toned conversation came over.

'But what can I say?' asked a voice in an excited whisper.

'Oh dear!' said the Owl Man, with a sigh. 'She's off again!'

She was!

'This is your Plainette speaking,' came next.

So it came about that as the great silver train slid over the last mile or two of its long journey, instead of the usual bustle and chatter on board there was a complete silence. For her passengers had all stopped doing whatever they were doing and were all listening intently to this song.

Now that we all are leaving Zephyr,
I'll say again,
That I am sure that I will neffer
Forget this lovely silver train.
And I hope we'll all remember
Ever so long
This lovely journey in September.
Please, too, remember this song.

All the time we keep on wishing,
Mary Plain and me,
That we were all not just finishing
Our Zephyr trip to the sea.

Ten · In which Mary helps to catch some crooks

THE Owl Man and Mary only stayed in San Francisco two days and then set off to Los Angeles by car, for they were going to spend a night in a Motel on the way which Otto's parents owned.

Mary had met Otto one Christmas at Worship's house and he and she had had an exciting adventure together, so she was looking forward to meeting him again.

'Why is it called a Motel instead of a Hotel?' she inquired.

'Because it's a small place where you can pull up for the night and have your car right outside the door.'

It did not seem an awfully good reason to Mary.

'This one is by the sea,' added the Owl Man.

'Why isn't it a Boatel, then?' asked Mary, rather too smartly.

The Owl Man thought it was time to change the subject, so he said, 'Look! There's the sea – the Pacific. Isn't it blue?'

It was, indeed; bright blue waves with huge white frills thundering on to the whitest sand Mary had ever seen. They drove along the road beside it for another half-hour and then they saw a big board which said 'PETUNIA MOTEL', and they turned off into a kind of big square yard with beds of petunia in it. Round three sides of it were built small one-roomed bungalows and each had its own front door and beside it a space for a car.

Otto rushed out, waving both arms. 'Gee! but it's good to see you again, kid,' he said, thumping Mary on the back. 'Meet my parents. Dad, this is Mary Plain and this is the Owl Man. How do, sir?'

Everybody shook hands all round and then after a few moments they moved into the Shaws' bungalow, where they had long iced drinks of lemon. Otto asked about Worship and all his grandchildren, but as soon as Mary had swallowed her drink he said he wanted to show her the sea and hurried her off. But when they had crossed the road he began to act in a very odd manner. He did not show Mary the sea at all but slipped into a kind of niche between two houses and sat down on a low wall there with his back to it. Mary squeezed in beside him. 'But you can't see the sea at all,' she objected.

'Don't want to. That was just an excuse to get out. Just you leave things to me, kid.'

Otto was very restless. No sooner had he settled himself on the wall than he got down again and, keeping flat against the side of the house, put his head round the corner and glanced up and down the road in each direction. He did not seem to want to talk but just went on sitting down and getting up again till Mary got sick of it. There he was again, flattened up against the house, like a pancake. What was he doing? She opened her mouth to ask, but at that very moment he shot back into the niche and, seizing Mary, pushed her behind him.

'Ssh!' he hissed into her ear. 'Don't dare move or speak. Just watch!'

Mary watched, but all she could see was Otto's back, so, despite his orders, she wriggled her head under his arm just in time to see a big yellow and

86

brown car swing into the entrance of the Motel opposite.

'See that!' gasped Otto.

'It's only a car,' said Mary, who had expected something really exciting like a circus or a runaway train or at least a procession.

'Only a car! Jehoshaphat!' exclaimed Otto. 'It's THEM! Listen, kid, while I let you in on this. I'm glad you're here because maybe you can help. Things have been disappearing out of the Motel, see? China, towels, blankets, etc., and I've got a hunch that the folks doing this pinching are the ones in that car right now. My Dad don't agree, but if I could catch them red-handed!'

'Do you mean bloody?' asked Mary, appalled.

'No, no, it's only an expression – means if I could catch them on the job with the things in the car, I'd be doing a real police job!'

The police sounded exciting and Mary's ears went up into points. 'But –' she began.

'Don't interrupt – just listen and maybe you can help me. Two's better than one and we've worked as a team before.'

'But –'

'Quit talking now. When everyone's in bed you can climb out of your window – you're in a slit of a room back of the Owl Man's. It won't be the first window you've climbed out of, will it?'

'No, but –'

'Listen! They won't make any move till after dark. It's about seven now. Directly after supper you say you're tired and get to bed right early and get some sleep. I'll come and wake you as soon as everything's quiet around. Got that straight?'

Mary nodded and before she could say 'but' again, Otto said, quickly, 'Fine! that's dandy,' and dashed back to the Motel with Mary behind him.

It all worked out according to plan. Before supper, Mary helped Mr Shaw water the petunias with a long hose and directly she had finished her supper she went off to bed and, tired after her long day, was tight asleep when Otto knocked three times on her window – which was the agreed signal.

It was a smallish window and Mary, who was not on the skinny side, had some difficulty in getting through, but at last, rather ruffled, she stood beside Otto on the tarmac.

Hand in paw they crept round the back of the rooms to the office by the entrance. It was a darkish night with only a dim light from a small neon-standard illuminating the yard. Otto drew Mary back into the shadow thrown by the wall and they sat down. Mary was glad to sit close beside him and glad he still held her paw, for her heart was going pit-a-pat. Her other side felt a bit lonely but, putting out her paw, she touched the little tap on the cold nozzle of the hose, still lying on the ground where Mr Shaw had dropped it. Mary held on to it – now she had something on both sides of her.

Suddenly, Otto gripped her other paw hard. 'Look!' he whispered. 'See, they're moving the car. They're pushing it out by hand so no one will hear them and I'm going to see what's in that car or bust. Stop here and guard the entrance – I'm off!' Bending low, he ran in the shadow round the edge of the square yard, towards the car.

Mary's right paw felt horribly lonely now, but she pushed back farther into the shadow and held tight on to the nozzle for company.

The car was being pushed very slowly – a man on each side. She could see Otto creeping along. Now he was level with the hood. Mary held her breath – if one of the men should turn his head! Now he was beyond the car. Suddenly, he shot out of the shadow to the back of the car. Gracious goodness! thought Mary, he'll be caught. Now, what was he doing? She could not see but she heard afterwards that he had hoisted himself on to the back of the car, looked through the window and there, as he had guessed, was a pile of pillows and two comforters on the seat.

The two men were so engrossed in steering the car that they did not look back and see Otto, nor did they hear him drop off and run soundlessly towards the alarm buzzer at the back of the yard.

As it pealed, the two men leapt away from the car and the one nearest Otto wheeled to run back to his room, but before he could start Otto flung himself against his legs and down he crashed, twisting his leg, and lay moaning, unable to move.

The second man made for the entrance. 'Stop him, kid! Stop him!' yelled Otto.

Mary sprang up, still grasping the hose. Quick as a flash she turned it on full and let the man have it right in his face, blinding him. He staggered, tripped over the hose and fell heavily, with Mary underneath him.

By this time, the Shaws and the Owl Man and all the other guests were pouring out of their rooms, trying in the dark to see what was happening. Mr Shaw ran to the light and turned it full on and then rushed towards his son who was standing over the first crook.

'I'm O.K.,' shouted Otto. 'His leg's broke, I think, and he can't move, but I think Mary's in trouble by the gate. Look's as if the chap's fallen on her. I guess he's about squashed her flat.'

At this grim announcement the Owl Man dashed towards the gate, prepared to do battle, but he found Mary sitting astride her victim's chest, leaning over his face with her teeth bared. Every time the man moved an eyelid she growled horribly.

She was very dishevelled, out of breath and pretty

bruised, but there was nothing squashed about her.

In wonderfully quick time, the police arrived. Their eyes fairly goggled when they saw the man they had been trying to catch for months in charge of one small bear.

Otto came up, still panting. 'Did it alone!' he gasped. 'She's some kid!'

'Some guy!' murmured the Inspector, looking with deep respect at Mary and keeping just out of her reach. 'You didn't do too badly yourself, son.'

'Oh that!' said Otto, embarrassed.

There was, however, no embarrassment about Miss Plain.

After a final very close lean and a last growl that nearly made her victim faint from shock, she sat upright on his chest and bowed a cool bow at the police.

'I'm not a guy, or a kid,' she announced. 'I'm Mary Plain, an unusual first-class bear from the bear-pits at Berne, and I've got a white rosette and a gold medal with a picture of myself on it. Did you know?'

'We didn't,' said the Inspector, and, with one accord the squad of six straightened up and gave Mary a fine salute.

'But we do now,' added the Inspector.

Eleven · Mary Plain to the rescue again

ON their first evening at Los Angeles an old friend of the Owl Man rang up and said she had several young visitors staying with her and they were all going for a picnic to Santa Monica the next day and would Mary like to come, too? He said indeed she would, so Mrs Grant said they would call for her at ten o'clock and the children would all be tickled to death to have a real bear as guest.

Next morning, Mary, with her suit-case in her paw, went down in good time to the hall to await their arrival. The case only had her bathing costume in it, but she had flatly refused to put it in a paper parcel. She said it was easier to carry it in the case and the Owl Man knew perfectly well why.

One day in the *Englandic* Mary had spent a happy hour pasting a strip of ship's labels round her case and the result had been most original – too original, the Owl Man thought.

Mrs Grant arrived very punctually, followed by four children who all stared hard at Mary.

'This is Robin and this is Barrie and the smaller ones are Sammy and James Ashby. So Mary will be the only girl and she'll have to distribute her favours fairly between them.'

'I haven't got any favours,' said Mary, 'but I'm pleased to meet you.' The two elder boys said they were sure pleased, too, but the two small ones just said 'Hi!'

In the car, examining the suit-case, all shyness soon wore off.

'It's the same ship in all the pictures,' said Barrie.

'Yes. You see, I only came in one ship,' explained Mary.

'Was it fun?' inquired Robin. Telling them what fun it had been lasted them till they got to the beach.

The nice part of a picnic at Santa Monica is that you can cook your food right on the shore in one of the dozens of concrete ovens which are built for that purpose. Mary had never been to that kind of a picnic before and was very puzzled.

'I like my sandwiches cold best, please,' she said to Mrs Grant, who had lit a fire in one of the ovens and placed a big pan on it.

'It isn't sandwiches, Mary,' she answered, taking off the lid. 'Take a look.'

So Mary looked and saw a lovely big chicken with a lot of vegetables and gravy around it.

'I've never been to a hot picnic before!' she said, giving a little hop because it smelt so good.

'What say we go take a dip while the chicken's heating?' suggested Robin and all the others chorused 'Yes!'

Now, Mary was very modest about some things and one of them was getting into her bathing costume. She looked around, but there were no rocks or bathing tents to be seen. In the end she explained to Mrs Grant, who very kindly held up a sun umbrella, which made an excellent private dressing-room for Mary.

All the children had nice swim-suits but none were as gay as Mary's bright red and white stripes. Except for James Ashby, who was too young to enjoy bath-

ing, they all dashed down to the sea and it was so lovely and warm that none of them took any time at all in getting wet all over.

Sammy wore water wings because he was only four, but Robin and Barrie could both swim a few strokes and Mary, of course, swam like a fish. She dived and swam under the water, turned somersaults and stood on her head and the boys were so interested watching her, and Mary so pleased at being watched, that none of them noticed that Sammy was kicking his way out to sea and was already several yards beyond the children. Luckily Mrs Grant turned round and saw him and rushed down to the sea calling, 'Sammy! Sammy! Come back! Sammy!'

Mary whirled about and, plunging in, set off as fast as she could go after him. Mrs Grant grabbed hold of Robin and Barrie, who both wanted to go to

the rescue, too, as she knew they were not yet strong enough swimmers to help.

Hearing the shouts, Sammy tried to turn and somehow his wings came off and he began to sink. But by this time Mary was near enough to mark the exact spot and one short dive was enough to get hold of him and pull him up. Poor Sammy had swallowed quite a lot of sea-water which frightened him and he began to struggle. Mary grabbed him firmly by the hair and gave him a little shake. 'Stop wriggling,' she cried, 'or I can't rescue you. Stop it now, or I'll push you under.'

At this dire threat, Sammy became as still as a dead fish and Mary said, 'Now take hold of my belt and I'll swim you in.'

This was easier said than done, for Sammy was no light weight and, by the time she reached the shore, poor Mary was pretty well puffed. Mrs Grant and the two boys waded out to meet her, shouting, 'Well done, Mary! Hurrah for Mary!' and dragged them in the last few yards.

Mary lay flat on her back, completely blown, but Sammy, after his dose of sea-water, coughed and spluttered and everyone fussed over them both. Robin, being the eldest, was especially impressed by Mary's behaviour and shook her warmly by the paw. 'You're a smart guy, Mary,' he said, 'and you deserve a medal.'

Mary stopped panting just long enough to say 'Got one!'

Directly Sammy could speak he said, 'Gee! I didn't know I was that far out. I guess Mary was swell to drag me all that way in. Thanks a lot, Mary.'

'You're welcome,' said Mary, who was becoming terribly American.

Robin was now sent flying to dip two cups into the strong chicken soup and both rescued and rescuer sat up and felt a lot better as the hot liquid trickled deliciously down their throats.

After lunch they all rested a bit and then, because Mrs Grant said positively no more bathing that day, they ran races and then built a big sand castle and Mary danced a jig on the top and sang 'I'm the King of the Castle!'

'How can you be King of the Castle, when you're a girl?' jeered Robin.

So Mary sang 'I'm the Plain of the Castle' instead and liked it much better and after that it was time to go home.

This was, however, not to be a lucky day for, on the way back, a car in front pulled up so suddenly that Mrs Grant had to jam on her brakes and Mary, who was sitting beside her in the front, was thrown against the windscreen so hard that she saw stars.

'Oh, my poor head,' she moaned, rubbing it, and when she took her paw down it was all red.

Now, Mary could not stand the sight of blood, especially her own, and when she saw her paw she let forth a loud wail.

Mrs Grant was most upset. She mopped at Mary's head and patted and stroked her and then had a look at the sore place which was difficult to find through the fur. 'It's not a bad cut, Mary,' she said, 'but I guess I'd better just run you into the hospital in case it needs a stitch.'

At this, Mary let out a longer and louder wail and only some chewing-gum produced by Robin stopped it. Even Mary could not successfully chew and wail at the same time.

As they approached the big white building, Mary's heart went pit-a-pat and it needed a lot of coaxing to get her out of the car on their arrival. Mrs Grant promised her a bag of candy if she was brave.

So when the surgeon, who was large and kind, said he 'guessed he'd have to put in a stitch', Mary set her teeth and thought so hard of the candy that it hardly hurt at all. The surgeon patted her on the side of her head that was not hurt and said she was the bravest and also the first bear he'd ever sewed up and she left the hospital with a cross of pink plaster which made her feel terribly important. Mrs Grant was so pleased with her that she bought her two bags of candy.

The Owl Man was near the hotel door when they got back and ran down the steps to meet them.

'Whatever's happened now?' he exclaimed as he saw Mary's plaster.

'Nothing serious – just a plasterectomy,' said Mrs Grant, quickly, 'and Mary was awfully brave.'

'And I'm not to take it off for a whole week!' said Mary triumphantly.

Twelve · Mary goes to Hollywood

THE Owl Man had an appointment with a director at Hollywood next day. He and Mary set out in a car soon after ten for the studios.

'What is Hollywood for?' inquired Mary, as they were whirled along the 'fabulous mile'.

'Well,' said the Owl Man, smiling, 'it's a place where they do cinema pictures.'

'Will they do me?' asked Mary eagerly.

'Good gracious me, no!' said the Owl Man, beginning to wish he had left Mary behind at the hotel. 'Now, look here, Mary, we must get this quite straight. I really ought not to have brought you at all but, as I have, you've got to be as quiet as a mouse and on your very best behaviour. And not speak unless you're spoken to. See?'

'But what happens if they don't speak to me?'

'Nothing. You just stay quiet.'

Mary sighed. Hollywood sounded horribly dull.

But when, after the talk, Mr Hart took them

behind the scenes to see the film he was directing and Mary saw the exciting hustle and bustle of a film set with voices shouting directions and everyone hurrying about under the great arc lamps, while the big cameras clicked, she changed her mind.

'What are you shooting?' inquired the Owl Man.

'Shooting!' gasped Mary, before she could stop herself and then clapped her paw over her mouth.

'Well,' said the director, who had not heard, 'it's a scene at a village fair. There are quite a number of side shows that give variety and actually,' he added, smiling down at Mary, 'there's a performing bear in one just due to rehearse now.'

It took both Mary's paws to keep her mouth shut this time.

'It's a bit worrying,' went on the director, 'for he's not used to performing, really, and he wasn't a very big success yesterday.'

This was too much. 'I am and I would be a huge one,' burst from Mary.

Mr Hart started. 'I didn't know it talked,' he said.

'Oh, yes! It talks all right,' said the Owl Man, dryly.

'Is that so? Please introduce me to –'

'Mary Plain. I'm an unusual first-class bear from the bear-pits at Berne and I've got a white rosette and a gold medal with a picture of myself on it.'

'Have you, indeed?' said Mr Hart. 'Well, I'm very pleased to meet you, Miss Plain. You certainly seem to be quite a personage. Excuse me one moment. What is it, Griffiths?' And he turned to speak to a man who was telling him something in a low tone.

'Won't come out of his stall?' exclaimed Mr Hart. 'But that won't do at all – he's got to come out. The whole scene will be wrecked without him – can't possibly – unless –' he stopped and looked at Mary. After thinking for a moment, he said, 'Miss Plain, see here! Our bear's in a bad mood and won't play. Do you think you could stand in for him?'

'Stand in what?' asked Mary, who liked to get things straight.

'That's just an expression we use – it means do his part-act.'

'What kind of an act?'

'Well, it's perfectly simple. He just walks across the village green and turns around and waves his arm a bit, I guess that's about all.'

'Pouf!' said Mary, dismissing the disagreeable bear with a wave of her paw. 'I can dance a ballet!'

'Is that so?' said the director, slowly, and he turned to the Owl Man with a gleam in his eye.

The Owl Man did his level best to discourage the gleam. 'I'm afraid it is,' he said, 'but look here, I do beg you to wait till your bear is available. I mean, you do know about him but you don't about Mary.'

All the time the director had been watching Mary, who, with her bright eyes darting everywhere, was on tip-paw with excitement.

'Of course, I appreciate I am a bit handicapped,' he admitted, 'for I don't know yet what you can do, Miss Plain. Suppose you show me? Right there in the centre of that patch of green.'

Miss Plain did not wait to be asked twice. In a flash she was out in the centre of the stage and had executed a pirouette when she pulled up short. 'I could pirouette better in a ballet frock,' she announced.

Mr Hart clapped his hands. 'A short ballet frock for Miss Plain, please,' he said and, in next to no time, Mary was wearing layer upon layer of blue net frills which the director thought were immensely becoming. Mary thought so, too.

She took up her position again and Mr Hart said 'Now!'

Mary did a beautiful sideways jump and then stopped again.

'Oh, Mary,' groaned the Owl Man, under his breath.

'I could jump better if I had a red rose behind my ear,' said Miss Plain.

'Let a red rose be fetched,' said Mr Hart and when it came he helped, with some difficulty, fix it behind Mary's left ear.

'Now!' said Mr Hart, again, very much hoping

that this time Mary would get on with the job. But after two *chassés* she stopped again.

'Where's the music?' she asked.

This seemed a very reasonable request, so a good record was chosen and this time Mary danced her dance all through. At the end, the director approached her no longer handicapped but, as it were, cap-in-hand. 'Fine!' he said, enthusiastically. 'First class and just what I wanted though I didn't know it! Could you just run through it once more so we can get the lighting adjusted before we shoot?'

'Me?' asked Mary, anxiously.

'Just another film expression,' laughed the director, patting her on the shoulder. 'Now, I want you to stand right there on the grass again while we get the lighting fixed.'

He gave a few orders and the electricians took over, moving various lamps up and down and around. Mary suddenly found herself standing in a patch of sunshine. 'Why! The sun's come out!' she exclaimed.

'Sure!' said the head lighting man with a grin.

Then it was the camera men's turn and, when the whole staff were as ready as they could be, Mr Hart said would Mary just run through the dance again to be sure they had the timing right.

After that, there was another pause while some final adjustments were made.

Then came the great moment.

'Ready, Miss Plain?' called Mr Hart. 'This is going to be great! You're going to give me more than I bargained for, I guess!'

He guessed right! Mary did.

When the word 'Shoot!' came Mary, in mid-stage, made a deep bow and said,

'I've never danced in Hollywood;
I hope you'll think I'm good.
In case you'd like my name to learn
I'm Mary Plain, the cub from Berne.'

Then she got on with the dance.

The Owl Man was red with annoyance and the director in despair. All my timing out of gear, he thought savagely and was just going to say 'Cut!' when Mary did a triple spin, so he stopped. And Mary chasséed and sprang and pirouetted even better than before, so the director still remained silent, and when at the end she sank to the grass in a final curtsy, leaving one paw in as near a point as she could manage out in front, he drew a deep breath and stroked his hair.

The Owl Man, who had been watching him anxiously, said, 'I'm awfully sorry, old man, but I did my best to warn you that you didn't know Mary.'

'But I believe I'm going to be mighty glad I do!' said Mr Hart.

Thirteen · Mary gives a press interview

THERE was a knock on the door of Mary's bedroom and the hotel manager came in. He was bald and he looked rather hot and bothered.

'I am glad to see you,' said Mary. 'I'm so tired of myself and the Owl Man has been gone such a long time.'

Actually, the Owl Man had gone just twenty minutes before, leaving the strictest orders that Mary was not to leave her room by the door or window during his absence.

'There are some gentlemen who would like a word with you,' said her visitor.

'Did you bring them?' asked Mary, trying to see round the manager, who was plump and blocked the doorway.

'Well, no,' he answered. 'I thought maybe you would come down to the Holbein Room?'

'But I promised the Owl Man to stay here,' said Mary, with great honesty. 'And,' she added, with even greater honesty, 'if I do, I'm to have two ice-cream sodas when he gets back – chocolate ones.' And she licked her lips.

'See here,' said the manager, mopping his brow with a large silk handkerchief. 'If you'll come down I'll put it right with the gentleman and you shall have three ice-cream sodas – all chocolate. There are round about forty press-men down there and I can't get rid of them,' he added, desperately.

'But I don't want to be pressed, thank you,' said Mary, drawing back.

'You mean you don't want your picture to be in the papers?'

'Is that what it means?'

'Sure!' said the manager.

Mary tucked her paw into his hand. 'I like being in papers,' she said, happily. 'I've got my best bow on – let's go.'

But even Mary was rather taken aback when they reached the Holbein Room. During the manager's absence more newspaper men and some women had arrived and it was filled from door to door. Everyone was talking at once and the hubbub was terrific.

The manager wanted to get Mary to a small platform at the farther end of the room, but the people were so tightly packed it was impossible to move. He clapped his hands for silence and said, 'Ladies and gentlemen! Please make way for Miss Plain, who, if she can reach the platform, has kindly consented to grant you all an interview.'

All the people, treading on each other's toes, squeezed themselves back and somehow a passage was made for Mary. She was so small that only the front row could see her and the others all craned their necks and some climbed up on chairs and window-sills to get a better view.

· To Mary, even a walk of a few yards with a crowd around her became a procession. So, while the manager hurried up the gangway, Mary, enjoying herself immensely, processed very slowly behind him, bowing from left to right as she went.

As the manager assisted her on to the platform a big cheer arose while flashlights flashed and cine-cameras clicked and whizzed.

Mary kept her head beautifully and did a bear bow

and the bow appeared next morning on the front page of all the Hollywood papers.

Pandemonium then broke loose, with everyone shouting questions at the same time, so that it was impossible to hear what they were asking. In the end, it was decided to toss as to who should begin and a beautiful blonde and a young journalist like a prize-fighter won and joined Mary on the platform.

'Is this your first visit to Hollywood?' asked the blonde.

'Yes,' said Mary. 'Shall I tell you my pome about it?'

One hundred and seventeen voices shouted 'Yes!' so Mary recited her 'pome' while all the biros got as busy as bees.

'Did you suffer from stage-fright?' inquired the prize-fighter.

'Pardon?' said Mary.

'Were you at all nervous on the set?'

'I didn't see any set,' said Mary, 'but, of course, I wasn't frightened, I'm used to doing things.'

'What kind of things?' inquired the blonde.

'Oh, concerts and shows and jubilees and bob-a-jobbing and aeroplaning and Zephyring.'

'Zephyring?' interrupted the journalist, while one hundred and seventeen biros remained hopefully poised.

'Yes, I've got a song about that,' said Mary and,

112

most obligingly, she sang it.

When the applause had died down the blonde asked, 'What is your favourite colour, Miss Plain?'

'Blue,' said Mary, 'like my bow. It makes me very smart, doesn't it?'

'It sure does,' said the journalist, 'and what do you like doing best?'

'Eating!' said Mary, frankly.

'And what is your favourite food?'

'Meringues and cream buns and ICE-CREAM

SODAS.' She said the last item very loudly, with an eye on the manager, who gave her a reassuring wave.

'And what would you say was the most exciting thing that ever happened to you?' asked the blonde.

'You mean next to Hollywood?' asked Mary, which remark brought a burst of cheering from her delighted listeners. She thought for a moment and then said 'Once I was napkinned.'

This time it was the blonde's turn to say 'Pardon?'

You could have heard a pin drop during Mary's description of how she had been kidnapped or 'napkinned', as she called it, and all the thrilling things that had happened to her before she had been rescued. Then she waved joyfully to the Owl Man, who had just appeared in the doorway.

The Owl Man waved much less joyfully back. Really, he couldn't go out for an hour without something happening to Mary – such public happenings, too. She seemed like a magnet to crowds.

Directly the manager saw the Owl Man, he pushed his way through towards him. He looked more hot and worried than ever as he explained what had occurred and how he had persuaded Mary to come down.

'I don't suppose she needed much persuading,' said the Owl Man, watching Mary, with newspaper men thronging round the platform, taking 'shots' from all angles, while the ladies stood around in admiring circles with their autograph books handy.

'Believe me,' said the manager, 'I had to work pretty hard to get her to come. It cost me three ice-cream sodas. They're coming up now. See?'

A bellboy with a tray was, indeed, to be seen, working his way up to the platform. Directly Mary saw him, she stopped talking and waved both arms, just in case he missed her. 'Here I am,' she cried, almost waving the tray out of his hands.

One journalist fetched a chair, another tucked his clean handkerchief around Mary's neck, while a third took the tray and, kneeling down, held it at a convenient angle. Several 'shots' were taken of this and the Owl Man shook his head and sighed. There'd be no holding Mary after this. When the third ice-cream soda was nearly finished, he pushed his way through the people and said, 'It's time to come now, Mary,' and he said it in the kind of voice that Mary knew it was best to obey, so she got up at once.

But a cry arose from the autograph hunters who all waved their books above their heads.

'All right,' said the Owl Man, resignedly, 'but hurry!'

So Mary signed her name one hundred and seventeen times, while the Owl Man stood on one foot and then on the other and tried hard not to wish he had left Mary in Berne where she really belonged. At last she had finished and they could leave, but just as they reached the door someone started singing, 'For she's a jolly good fellow!' The Owl Man played up and swung Mary on his shoulder so they could all have a last look.

'Three cheers for the newest Hollywood star!' shouted one man and the Owl Man ground his teeth in despair.

But he need not have worried.

Late that evening, when he went in to say 'Good night' to Mary, he found her leaning out of the window.

'What are you looking at, Mary?' he asked.

'I'm trying to find the new star,' she said. 'Can you see it, Owl Man?'

The Owl Man ruffled her head and said, 'It was a pretty small star. I expect it's gone to bed.'

Fourteen · Good-bye to USA

BACK in New York, Mary and the Owl Man had just twenty-four hours before they sailed. He had promised her that she should go up the Empire State Building before they left and see the illuminations. So, on their last evening, they set out.

When the elevator reached the fiftieth floor, Mary began to look anxious. 'Are we going through the roof?' she asked.

The liftman laughed as he pulled up at the eightieth floor and said he 'guessed not – she still had another thirty floors to go in another elevator and after that some stairs.'

When at last they emerged on the sloping platform that encircles the top of the building, a high wind was blowing and the Owl Man held Mary's paw tight while she peeped over the edge and saw, way below, the huge glittering carpet of lights that was New York.

'Are we in the sky?' she asked, and the Owl Man said, 'Pretty near.'

The two great rivers were like arms cradling the sparkling city and the Owl Man pointed out the *Englandic* lying at her pier.

'Have you the correct time?' inquired a voice from behind, and to get out his watch the Owl Man let go of Mary's paw. By the time he had put it back, she had disappeared.

'Mary! Mary!' he called urgently, looking around, and he was just going to call again when he caught his breath. For Mary had wanted a better view of the *Englandic* and, to get it, she was standing on the parapet, swaying in the wind with nothing in front of her but New York, thousands of feet below.

The Owl Man moved as swiftly and as quietly as he could and he had got within a few feet when Mary called excitedly, 'Look! There's our ship, just down there!'

She pointed with her paw and a gust of wind made her sway so dangerously that the Owl Man jumped the remaining two yards, caught her round the middle and swept her back, only just in time.

Neither could speak for a moment and then a voice said, 'Gee! That was a near shave!'

The Owl Man, who still could not speak, turned and saw the young fellow who had asked him the time standing beside them with a small boy in tow.

'Hallo, bear!' said the child.

'Hallo, boy!' said Mary.

'I'm Alexander. Isn't it a long name?'

'I'm Mary Plain-an-unusual-first-class-bear-from-the-bear-pits-at-Berne,' said Mary, saying it all in one so as to be longer than Alexander. 'And I've got a white rosette and a gold medal with a picture of myself on it. Have you?'

'Well, no,' said Alexander, slowly, 'but I've got a white mouse without a tail down home.'

'So have –'

'Mary, Mary!' interrupted the Owl Man, who had just got his breath back.

Mary hung her head.

'See here!' said the father, 'you two get inside out of this wind and go to the stall and buy yourselves each a present,' and he handed Mary and Alexander a dollar apiece.

'Oh, thank you!' said Mary, who had never had a piece of paper money before, and while the Owl Man was thanking the kind father, his son said 'Come along on!' and dragged Mary off to the shop.

When the grown-ups joined them a few moments later, they had finished their shopping. Alexander was holding a jack-knife with a coloured picture of the Empire State Building on it, while Mary was resplendent in a shirt a size too big, with pictures of New York painted all over it.

'Oh, no, Mary!' exclaimed the Owl Man.

'Oh, yes, Owl Man, please,' said Mary. 'Just look! Here's the building we're on top of, on my front. Isn't it exciting? And on my back too,' and she turned round.

'I'm afraid it's all my fault,' said the young American, 'and I guess you'll have to bear it!'

The Owl Man laughed. After all, he was used to bearing things about Mary. He did, however, insist that Mary carried it back to the hotel in a parcel and not on her person.

He had been a little nervous lest the news of Mary's appearance in Hollywood should have reached New York, so, on arriving at the pier next morning, he kept a wary eye about him, but no journalists seemed to be about.

Just as they were stepping on to the gangway, however, a rather embarrassed young man rushed up to Mary, thrust a huge bunch of flowers into her arms and rushed away again. There was a card attached on which was written. 'Bon voyage to Miss Mary Plain. Come again soon. From all her American fans.'

'What are fans?' inquired Mary.

'Er – just another name for friends,' said the Owl Man.

'What friends?' asked Mary next, but the Owl Man did not answer and, after all, what did it matter? What did matter was that when Mary boarded the *Englandic* you could hardly see her for orchids and the crew had to welcome her back over the top of them.

They all seemed delighted to see her. The Chief Purser said he hoped Mary had some new songs to sing to them and Mary was just going to oblige with her Zephyr song when the Owl Man hurried her off.

On their way down they met the Captain. 'Here

comes the bride!' he quoted, laughing at Mary's sheath, but it was a kind laugh. 'We'll have to have a celebration one night,' he said, 'and think up a farewell entertainment, eh, Miss Plain?'

'And I can dance my Hollywood ballet and sing my new songs and say my new pome,' said Miss Plain, through the orchids. She had to say most of it backwards over her shoulder as the Owl Man was hustling her down to their cabin.

It was the same one which they had had on the trip out and it was full of 'sailing presents'. The Grants had sent a big box of candy and Missy and Rosamund a jar of maple syrup and Alexander a dear little ornament of the Empire State Building with jelly beans inside.

Mary was thrilled. 'And I've got two more on my shirt,' she exclaimed and insisted on unfastening her case and showing the steward.

By the time they had got straight it was time to sail. 'I'm going up to see the last of New York, Mary,' said the Owl Man. 'Slip out of that shirt and come and join me on the Promenade deck.'

Mary somehow forgot to slip and when she joined the Owl Man she was still in the shirt and still held her flowers. But you could really see so little of Mary behind them that he let the shirt pass and they went up into the stern and watched the sailors casting off the ropes and the gangways being hauled off and all the bustle and flurry of departure.

The pier dock was built in so you could not see any people waving 'good-bye', but there was plenty else to see and hear as the big ship nosed her way out into mid-river and turned towards the waiting ocean.

At first, the sky-scrapers towered beside them and then, as they got farther and farther away, they faded into the blue distance till at last New York looked like a tiny fairy city rising out of the sea.

A woman standing beside them turned to the Owl Man and said, 'I've seen New York disappear many times but it never fails to move me. It's a wonderful sight – all that soaring sky-line against the blue sky.'

Mary had never seen it before. Her good-bye was much shorter and the Owl Man liked it best.

'Good-bye, Usa,' she said.

These are other Knight Books

LION AT LARGE
Richard Parker

No one believes Barry when he says
he saw a lion in the garden, and he
begins to think he imagined it. Then he and
Ingrid find the lion, injured after a circus
fire. Feeding it is a problem, but a greater
problem arises when the meat they gave
it restores the lion to bounding energy!
'A beauty – extremely well-written,
utterly fantastic and yet, in fact,
completely possible!'
BBC Children's Hour
Illustrated by Paul Hogarth

MEET THE PEANUTS GANG

DON'T TREAD ON
CHARLIE BROWN
Charles M. Schulz

If you haven't met the Peanuts gang
before, now's your chance to get
acquainted with Charlie Brown and his
friends (not forgetting Snoopy the dog)
who have made such a hit in this
country and the United States. And if you
are already a Peanuts fan, these books
contain some of the earlier cartoons
which you probably won't have seen before.

These are other Knight Books

THE SPLENDID JOURNEY
Honore Morrow

'. . . a tall boy, thin as a shadow, his ragged red shirt tied up with bits of rope to keep it from dropping altogether from his body, his feet wrapped with strips of oxhide, a boy whose long hair fell over his shoulders and whose blue eyes were startlingly large and clear in his tanned face.'

This is John Sager, described during his long journey along the Oregon trail, with his younger brothers and sisters. Set in the America of the 1840's this story is founded on fact.

THE MOFFATS
Eleanor Estes

The Moffats, Rufus, Sylvie, Joey, Jane and Mama – live in the yellow house on New Dollar Street, and their adventures and escapades in the small town of Cranbury have delighted several generations of children since they were first published in America.

'This author has a crisp certainty, a neat turn of phrase and a real sense of childhood pleasures. It's a joy to welcome an overseas visitor who has so much to offer us.'
Margery Fisher

THE SPETTECAKE HOLIDAY

Edith Unnerstad

Pelle Göran goes to live with his grandmother while his mother is in hospital. Also staying at Grandmother's is Kaja, and together they spend the most wonderful summer imaginable on the farm in southern Sweden.

'This delightful book seems to have all the elements – edible, scenic and ethical – that an eight- or nine-year-old could desire in a tale.'
Naomi Lewis in *The Observer*

Awarded the Nils Holgersson prize, given by Swedish librarians for the best children's book of 1957.
